tarrington

April
Bubbles
Chocolate

An
ABC
of Poetry

Selected by Lee Bennett Hopkins
Illustrated by Barry Root

Simon & Schuster Books for Young Readers
Published by Simon & Schuster
New York   London   Toronto   Sydney   Tokyo   Singapore

Contents

APRIL

Green blades of grass,
Yellow crocus shoots.

Grow high, bright flowers;
Go deep, dark roots.

Goodbye, snow boots!

Eve Merriam

BUBBLES

Two bubbles found they had rainbows on their curves.
They flickered out saying:
"It was worth being a bubble just to have held that
  rainbow thirty seconds."

Carl Sandburg

CHOCOLATE

Chocolate
Chocolate

        i
love
    you so
       i
want
   to
marry
    you
    and
live
   forever
      in the
      flavor
of your
  brown

Arnold Adoff

DREAMS

Hold fast to dreams
For if dreams die
Life is a broken-winged bird
That cannot fly.

Hold fast to dreams
For when dreams go
Life is a barren field
Frozen with snow.

Langston Hughes

ELEPHANT

The elephant carries a great big trunk.
He never packs it with clothes.
It has no lock and it has no key,
But he takes it wherever he goes.

Anonymous

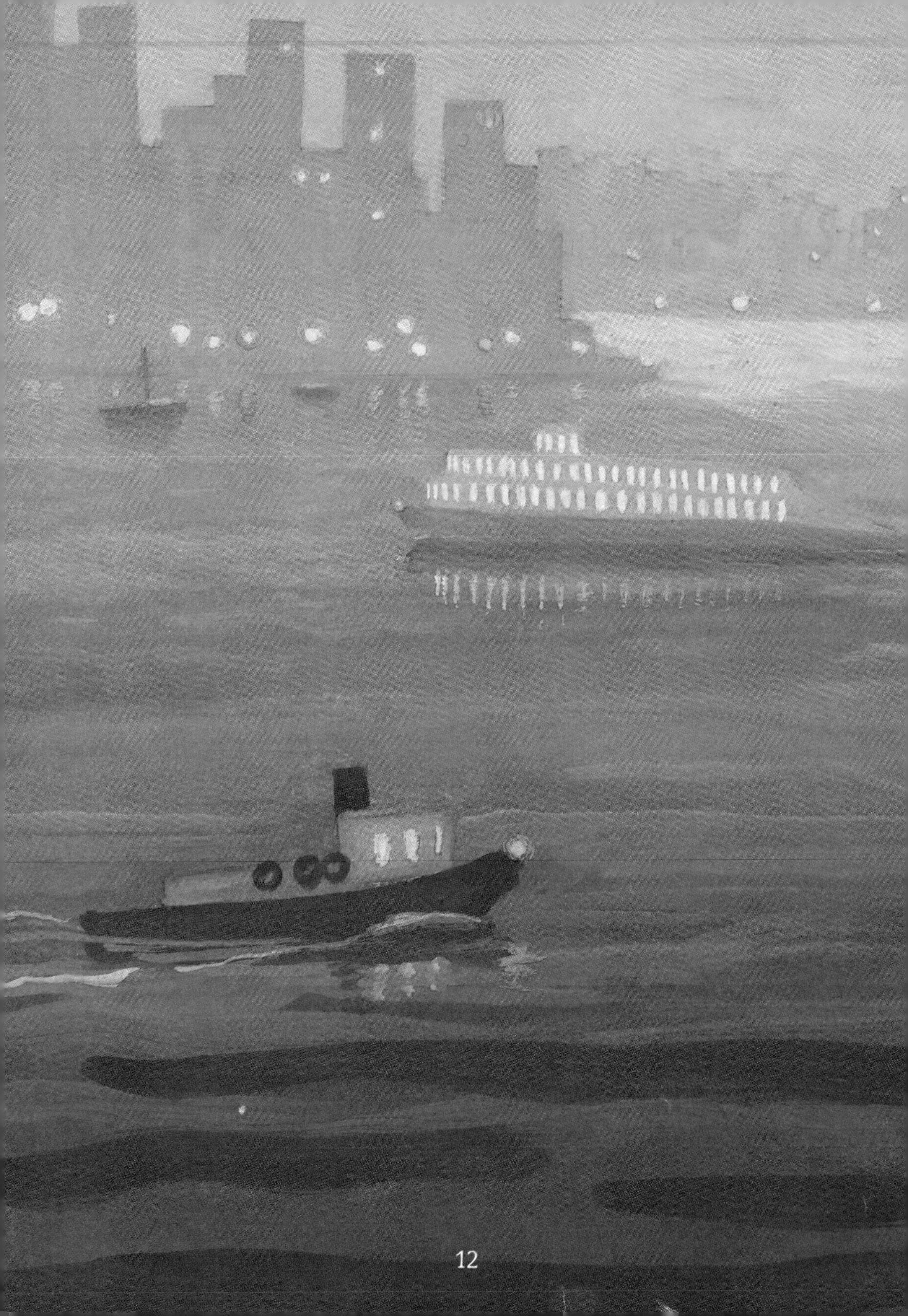

FOGHORNS

The foghorns moaned
        in the bay last night
    so sad
    so deep
I thought I heard the city
        crying in its sleep.

Lilian Moore

GRASSHOPPER

He's a happy-go-hopper,
A green garden guy,
With his zigzag legs
And his knees so high,

With his legs at the ready,
Set to bounce like a ball—
He looks like he's hopping
When he *isn't* at all.

Beverly McLoughland

HAPPY HALLOWEEN

It's late and we are sleepy,
The air is cold and still.
Our jack-o'-lantern grins at us
Upon the window sill.

We're stuffed with cake and candy
And we've had a lot of fun,
But now it's time to go to bed
And dream of all we've done.

We'll dream of ghosts and goblins
And of witches that we've seen,
And we'll dream of trick-or-treating
On this happy Halloween.

Jack Prelutsky

ICICLES

Have you tasted icicles
fresh from the edge
of the roof?

Have you let the sharp ice
melt
in your mouth
like cold swords?

The sun plays them
like a glass
xylophone   a crystal
harp.

All day they fall
chiming
into the pockmarked
snow.

Barbara Juster Esbensen

JACK-O'-LANTERN

Jack-o'-lantern, Jack-o'-lantern,
orange-front-and-back-o'-lantern,
sitting-on-the-sill-o'-lantern,
where's your sister Jill-o'-lantern?

Aileen Fisher

KITTEN

My gray kitten
Is clean because
She washed her fur
And all her paws.

And I know the words
Of the song she sung
After she washed
With her pink tongue.

Purr-purr, purr-purr,
Purr-purr, purr!
    Purr-purr, purr-purr,
    Purr-purr, purr!

James S. Tippett

LASAGNA

Wouldn't you love
To have lasagna
Any old time
The mood was on ya?

X. J. Kennedy

MOON

Moon
Have you met my mother?
Asleep in a chair there
Falling down hair.

Moon in the sky
Moon in the water
Have you met one another?
Moon face to moon face
Deep in that dark place
Suddenly bright.

Moon
Have you met my friend the night?

Karla Kuskin

NOW

Close the barbecue.
Close the sun.
Close the home-run games we won.

Close the picnic.
Close the pool.

Close the summer.

Open school.

Prince Redcloud

THE OCTOPUS

Tell me, O Octopus, I begs,
Is those things arms, or is they legs?
I marvel at thee, Octopus;
If I were thou, I'd call me Us.

Ogden Nash

PIE

After the yellow-white
Pie dough is rolled out
Flat, and picked up
Drooping like a round
Velvet mat, fitted gently
Into the dish, and piled
With sliced, sugared,
Yellow-white apples,
Covered with still another
Soft dough-blanket,
The whole thing trimmed
And tucked in tight, then
It is all so neat, so
Thick and filled and fat,
That we could happily
Eat it up, even
Before it is cooked.

Valerie Worth

QUIET

QUIET
  it says
  in the library
QUIET

  and what I want to know is

  what's quiet
  inside the books
  with all those
  ideas and words
  SHOUTING?

Myra Cohn Livingston

RACCOON

Raccoon,
with your black ringed eyes
and tiny paws,
startled at your work,
to you my garbage can
is full
of treasure.

Charlotte Zolotow

SNOW

Softly
whitely
down
the snow
mounds
and sifts
in dunes
in drifts
coldly
sowing
fields
of clover
covering
December
over.

Felice Holman

TUNNEL

Tunnel in the park:
a sandwich of night between
two slices of light

Sylvia Cassedy

UNTIL

Until
the new
hose
is
connected
there
is
so
much
use
for
that treasured
old-weathered
watering
can.

Lee Bennett Hopkins

VALENTINES

Forgive me if I have not sent you
a valentine
but I thought you knew
that you already have my heart
Here take the space where my
heart goes
I give that to you too

Henry Dumas

WASPS

Wasps like coffee.
Syrup.
Tea.
Coca-Cola.
Butter.
Me.

Dorothy Aldis

XEROX CANDY BAR

Ah,
you're just a copy
of all the candy bars
I've ever eaten.

Richard Brautigan

YELLOW

Green is go,
and red is stop,
and yellow is peaches
with cream on top.

Earth is brown,
and blue is sky;
yellow looks well
on a butterfly.

Clouds are white,
black, pink, or mocha;
yellow's a dish of
tapioca.

David McCord

ZEBRA

white sun
black
fire escape,

morning
grazing like a zebra
outside my window.

Judith Thurman

ACKNOWLEDGMENTS

Every effort has been made to trace the ownership of all copyrighted material and to secure necessary permissions to reprint these selections. In the event of any question arising as to the use of any material, the editor and the publisher, while expressing regret for any inadvertent error, will be happy to make the necessary correction in future printings. Thanks are due to the following for permission to reprint the copyrighted materials listed below:

The Helen Brann Agency, Inc. for "Xerox Candy Bar" from *The Pill Versus the Springhill Mine Disaster* by Richard Brautigan. Copyright © 1989 by Richard Brautigan. Reprinted by permission of The Helen Brann Agency, Inc. / Curtis Brown, Ltd. for "Until" by Lee Bennett Hopkins. Copyright © 1984 by Lee Bennett Hopkins. Reprinted by permission of Curtis Brown, Ltd. / Henry Dumas for "Valentines" from *Play Ebony, Play Ivory* (Random House). / Farrar, Straus & Giroux, Inc. for "Pie" from *Small Poems* by Valerie Worth. Copyright © 1972 by Valerie Worth. Reprinted by permission of Farrar, Straus & Giroux, Inc. / Aileen Fisher for "Jack-O'-Lantern" from *Runny Days, Sunny Days*. Used by permission of the author, who controls all rights. / Harcourt Brace Jovanovich, Inc. for "Bubbles" from *Wind Song* by Carl Sandburg. Copyright © 1960 by Carl Sandburg and renewed 1988 by Margaret Sandburg, Janet Sandburg, and Helga Sandburg Crile; "Raccoon" from *Everything Glistens and Everything Sings* by Charlotte Zolotow. Copyright © 1987 by Charlotte Zolotow. Both reprinted by permission of Harcourt Brace Jovanovich, Inc. / HarperCollins Publishers for "Icicles" from *Cold Stars and Fireflies: Poems of the Four Seasons* by Barbara Juster Esbensen. Text copyright © 1984 by Barbara Juster Esbensen; "Kitten" from *Crickety Cricket!: The Best Loved Poems of James S. Tippett* by James Tippett. Copyright 1933, copyright renewed © 1973 by Martha K. Tippett; "Moon" from *Dogs & Dragons, Trees & Dreams* by Karla Kuskin. Copyright © 1980 by Karla Kuskin; "Tunnel" from *Roomrimes* by Sylvia Cassedy. Text copyright © 1987 by Sylvia Cassedy. All reprinted by permission of HarperCollins Publishers. / Felice Holman for "Snow" from *I Hear You Smiling and Other Poems*, Charles Scribner's Sons, 1973. Used by permission of the author, who controls all rights. / Alfred A. Knopf, Inc. for "Dreams" from *The Dream Keeper and Other Poems* by Langston Hughes. Copyright 1932 by Alfred A. Knopf, Inc., renewed 1960 by Langston Hughes. Reprinted by permission of the publisher. / Little, Brown and Company for "The Octopus" from *Verses from 1929 On* by Ogden Nash. Copyright 1942 by Ogden Nash. First appeared in the *New Yorker*; "Yellow" from *One at a Time* by David McCord. Copyright © 1974 by David McCord. Both reprinted by permission of Little, Brown and Company. / Macmillan Publishing Company for "Foghorns" from *Something New Begins* by Lilian Moore. Copyright © 1969, 1982 by Lilian Moore. Reprinted with permission of Macmillan Publishing Company; excerpt from "Lasagna" from *Ghastlies, Goops & Pincushions* by X. J. Kennedy. Copyright © 1979, 1989 by X. J. Kennedy. Reprinted with permission of Margaret K. McElderry Books, an imprint of Macmillan Publishing Company. / Beverly McLoughland for "Grasshopper." Used by permission of the author, who controls all rights. / William Morrow and Company for an excerpt from "Lovesong" from *Eats* by Arnold Adoff. Copyright © 1979 by Arnold Adoff. By permission of Lothrop, Lee & Shepard Books, a division of William Morrow & Company, Inc.; "Happy Halloween" from *It's Halloween* by Jack Prelutsky. Copyright © 1977 by Jack Prelutsky. By permission of Greenwillow Books, a division of William Morrow & Company, Inc. / The Putnam Publishing Group for "Wasps" from *Is Anybody Hungry?* by Dorothy Aldis. Copyright © 1964 by Dorothy Aldis. By permission of G. P. Putnam's Sons. / Prince Redcloud for "Now." Used by permission of the author, who controls all rights. / Marian Reiner for "April" from *There Is No Rhyme for Silver and Other Poems* by Eve Merriam. Copyright © 1962 by Eve Merriam. Copyright © renewed 1990 by Eve Merriam; "Quiet" from *The Malibu and Other Poems* by Myra Cohn Livingston. Copyright © 1972 by Myra Cohn Livingston; "Zebra" from *Flashlight and Other Poems* by Judith Thurman. Copyright © 1976 by Judith Thurman. All reprinted by permission of Marian Reiner for the authors.

SIMON & SCHUSTER BOOKS FOR YOUNG READERS

Simon & Schuster Building, Rockefeller Center, 1230 Avenue of the Americas, New York, New York 10020.

The illustrations were done in watercolor. Manufactured in the United States of America.

10 9 8 7 6 5 4 3 2 1

Library of Congress Cataloging-in-Publication Data

April, bubbles, chocolate / [compiled] by Lee Bennett Hopkins ; illustrated by Barrett Root.   p.   cm.
Summary: A collection of poems on things from A to Z, by such authors as Eve Merriam, Carl Sandburg, and Arnold Adoff.   1. Children's poetry, American.   2. English language—Alphabet—Juvenile literature. [1. American poetry—Collections. 2. Alphabet.]   I. Hopkins, Lee Bennett.   II. Root, Barrett, ill.   III. Title.
PS586.3.A67   1994   811.088'09282—dc20   [E]   92-17100   CIP   ISBN: 0-671-75911-6